Let's Play Outside

By Pat Rumbaugh

Photographs by Daniel Nakamura

STAR BRIGHT BOOKS

CAMBRIDGE MASSACHUSETTS

Published in the US by Star Bright Books, Inc.
The name Star Bright Books and the Star Bright Books logo
are registered trademarks of Star Bright Books, Inc.

Please visit: www.starbrightbooks.com. For orders,
email: orders@starbrightbooks.com or call: (617) 354-1300.

Hardcover ISBN: 978-1-59572-918-7
Paperback ISBN: 978-1-59572-919-4
Star Bright Books / MA / 00106210
Printed in China / WKT / 9 8 7 6 5 4 3 2 1

Printed on paper from sustainable forests.

Library of Congress Cataloging-in-Publication Data

Names: Rumbaugh, Pat, author. | Nakamura, Daniel, 1979- illustrator.
Title: Let's play outside / by Pat Rumbaugh ; photographs by Daniel
  Nakamura.
Description: Cambridge, Massachusetts : Star Bright Books, 2021. |
  Audience: Ages 4-8. | Audience: Grades K-1. | Summary: "With this book,
  youngsters can discover many different ways to enjoy the outside-at a
  playground, in a park, in safe neighborhood streets, or in one's own
  backyard- including running, biking, swinging, hula-hooping, doing
  handstands, and exploring. Featuring bright photos of children in motion
  from mixed backgrounds and abilities"-- Provided by publisher.
Identifiers: LCCN 2021005048 | ISBN 9781595729187 (hardcover) | ISBN
  9781595729194 (paperback)
Subjects: CYAC: Outdoor recreation--Fiction. | Play--Fiction.
Classification: LCC PZ7.1.R856 Le 2021 | DDC [E]--dc23
LC record available at https://lccn.loc.gov/2021005048

To family and friends who join me outside to play.

—Love, Pat, The Play Lady

To my daughters Emily and Natalie who inspire me to always find time to play. I love you.

—Daniel

Playing outside
is a lot of fun!

Playing outside
makes us happy.

Playing outside
makes us strong.

We make new friends
when we play outside.

Let's play outside on a swing.
I can almost touch the sky!

Let's play outside on a slide.
I go down faster than a roller coaster!

Let's play outside on a climbing net. One big step at a time and I can reach to the top.

Let's play outside doing handstands.
One foot in front, hands to the ground, and
kick up the legs! It takes a lot of practice.

Let's play outside on the monkey bars. Grip one bar, swing the legs, and move to the next! I feel powerful.

Jumping rope to one hundred is a blast!

Hula-hooping
together is a hoot!

You jump, I hop on
a hopscotch square!

I soar, you fly on a seesaw!

Let's spin the roundabout.
Everyone gets a turn.

Let's follow the leader.
It's fun for everyone.

Let's play outside on wheels. We are going to the moon!

Let's play outside with a ball.
I believe I can do anything!

Playing outside with friends is fun.

Playing outside by myself is fun too!

Let's play out**side!**

Playing Outside: A Lifetime Gift for Your Child

Children are born curious and adventurous; they are risk takers and enthusiastic copycats. If a child sees another child playing with a ball, then they too want to play with a ball. If a child sees a child go down a slide, then they want to go down a slide.

When children are outside their choices of play multiply: climbing, jumping, throwing balls, running, swinging, and playing games not suitable for indoor play. Children naturally want to climb trees, ride their bikes or wheelchairs as fast as they can, and play all sorts of games.

Not all children are alike, but all children do love to play. One of the biggest gifts you can give a child is the gift of play, especially outside activities that are age-appropriate and child-driven.

Learning through Play
Playing games and activities outside is a great way for children to develop all kinds of skills. For instance, while playing hopscotch, a child learns math and develops physical skills. Playing follow-the-leader or Simon Says helps children build listening skills and learn to follow directions.

Playing together also has benefits. Children learn to get along and cooperate with each other. Older children show more empathy when playing with younger children; younger children expand their vocabulary by being around older children.

Children also benefit from playing outside with adults and caregivers. Adults can teach children new skills such as kicking a soccer ball or spinning a hoop. Adults who model positive behaviors and words show children to be respectful of others and play fairly. Encouragement and patience help children feel confident and equipped to try new experiences.

Some children are happy playing on their own. They can choose whether or not they want to participate in group play.

A Healthy, Happy, and Resilient Child
In the last two decades, there has been a major decline in the time children play outside. Research shows that children are less active today due to the ubiquitous presence of TV, smartphones, tablets, and other screens. Anxiety and depression in children have also subsequently increased.

When children have opportunities for physical activities and adequate time to play outside, they are more physically fit, less stressed, and emotionally and socially healthier. Their imaginations soar in a nature-based environment—with dirt, trees, and water. Playing with other children in a relaxed atmosphere helps develop social-emotional skills.

Play is magical. Together, you and your child can create many happy memories!

Visit the Let's Play America's website:
www.letsplayamerica.org

Play Tips for Caregivers and Parents

Be Kind and Respectful to Everyone

Before playtime, discuss these simple principles for play so everyone can have fun:

- Invite other children to play and share your toys.
- Everyone takes a turn when playing together.
- Ask politely if you would like to play with someone else's toys.

Let your child know how long they will be allowed to play and give them a five-minute warning when playtime is almost over.

Safety

It is important that children have the opportunity to take risks when they play, but there are certain safety rules to explain beforehand:

- Do not push or hurry others while on playground equipment. Wait for your turn.
- Stand in a safe place when waiting for your turn on the swing.
- Leave bikes and backpacks out of the play area.
- Always wear a helmet while riding a bike, but take it off while on playground equipment.

All children play differently. Caregivers can observe patterns in children's play activities and respond appropriately. For example, if you have a high-energy little girl who wants to keep up with her big brother and can't help herself, tend to her closely to ensure she doesn't overdo it. Once she has established that she can play safely on her own, watch from a distance. This can be a balancing act for caregivers.

Fitting in Time to Play

Children need daily opportunities to be physically active outside. Young children should have a minimum of one hour outside play every day. Find a time that fits your child's daily routine.

- Can your child play at the school playground, at a local park, or in the backyard after school? This time is special for children because they have likely been in an adult-led setting most of the day.
- Weekend playtime is important. Going to their favorite park or playing outside with a friend can be the highlight of a child's day.
- Family playtime outside is also important. Take turns choosing a family outdoor activity.
- Playing with relatives can be a special occasion or a weekly activity. Young children benefit from spending time with extended family.

Places to Play

Children and their families are more likely to play in areas within a fifteen-minute walk of their homes like outside parks and playgrounds. But there are other creative ways to find safe places for children to play:

- Some school playgrounds might be open to the public on evenings and weekends.
- Check for local businesses with open parking areas.
- Can a street be closed every Saturday or Sunday morning for three hours, for children to play?
- Consider inviting neighborhood children over to play in the backyard, in the driveway, or on play equipment in your yard.